bad machinery

THE CASE OF THE LONELY ONE

AN ONI PRESS PUBLICATION

CRUNCH
CRUNCH
TAP
TAP

bad machinery

THE CASE OF THE LONELY ONE

by
John Allison

Edited by
Ari Yarwood

Designed by
Hilary Thompson

PUBLISHED BY ONI PRESS INC.
founder & chief financial officer, **Joe Nozemack**
publisher, **James Lucas Jones**
v.p. of creative & business development, **Charlie Chu**
director of operations, **Brad Rooks**
marketing manager, **Rachel Reed**
publicity manager, **Melissa Meszaros**
director of design & production, **Troy Look**
graphic designer, **Hilary Thompson**
junior graphic designer, **Kate Z. Stone**
digital prepress lead, **Angie Knowles**
executive editor, **Ari Yarwood**
senior editor, **Robin Herrera**
associate editor, **Desiree Wilson**
administrative assistant, **Alissa Sallah**
logistics associate, **Jung Lee**

ONI PRESS

onipress.com
facebook.com/onipress
twitter.com/onipress
onipress.tumblr.com
instagram.com/onipress
scarygoround.com

FIRST EDITION: OCTOBER 2015
POCKET EDITION: MARCH 2018

ISBN 978-1-62010-457-6
EISBN 978-1-62010-213-8

PRINTED IN CHINA.

LIBRARY OF CONGRESS CONTROL NUMBER: 2017949448

1 2 3 4 5 6 7 8 9 10

SHAUNA

LOTTIE

MILDRED

JACK

LINTON

SONNY

At the publisher's request, all references to "Super Derek" have been removed from the following story.

4
MON
OCTOBER

CLACK
CLACK

HUFF
PUFF
HUFF
PUFF

Please... come on... YOU wouldn't do this to me!

Of everyone it could be!

NOT YOU!

1

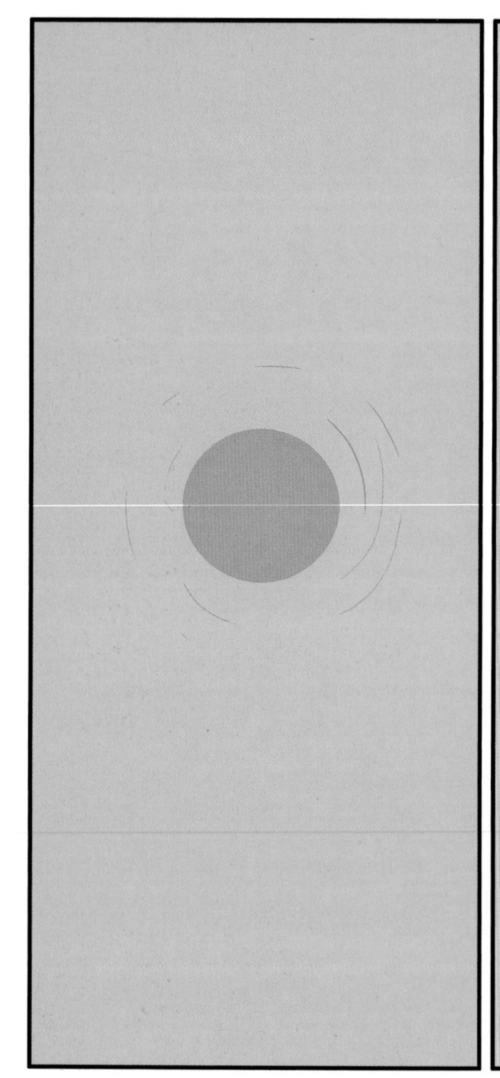

3
FRI
SEPTEMBER

Corrrr!

They're so new, so precious... they don't really have personalities yet!

I just want to dress them up and make them dance and-
Lottie, leave the new first years alone!

Let's sniff the tops of their heads.
They might still have the new baby smell!

Can I adopt one?
NO.
I want one too! Like a cross between a golf caddy and a slave.

Where am I?
I'm not in your class!
They put everyone doing Latin in the same class.
FORM

But I didn't know! I didn't *realise*!
Come on Lottie, it'll be all right.

Don't start your 2nd year by crying.
Come on.

You're ALL in the same class! Jack, Sonny, even Linton!

Linton only did it because his name almost sounds like "Latin".

CHRIST ON THE PROVERBIAL FLIPPING BIKE!

I'm in 2L. 2L? Mrs Lord? Who's Mrs Lord?
There are nice people in that class. Neil... Kitty Winkleton...
...Little Claire's... *all right*...

Don't worry Lotthie.
TWINK

We will thtick together!
BOTHOM FRIENDTH!
Let'th have a THLEEP OVER!

I CAN'T TAKE...
...SIX YEARS...
...SITTING NEXT TO LITTLE CLAIRE...

Lottie, you know there was a form you had to fill in if you chose Latin?

A form... a form...
RUMMAGE

OH.
GRISWALDS GRAMMAR
OH Boy
FARTZILLA
Dear Parent
Please sign the tear-off form below to confirm that your child wishes to continue with Latin in the second year.
Sincerely,
R. Spink
PUMP
MORE BEANS MAN

I'm a bit nervous about being in Mr Spink's class.
He's a man of DISCIPLINE and FURY.

Miss Grote, why are you loitering in my portal?
MATHS

Um I forgot to apply to be in this class but-

Your marks were not thought to be... *Latin class material.*
No but-

YOU'RE NOT ON YOUR DADDY'S YACHT NOW, TWINKLE!
SHRED

SKITTER SKITTER

THE ANCIENT WORLD

That girl can certainly shift when startled.
Arthurs!
SIR!
Baxter!
SIR!
Craven!
SIR!

Bad Machinery, Volume Four

Who's that kid?
He's in my class. He's new.

It must be hard not knowing anyone, when everyone else knows each other.
TWIST

Well, he's a boy. It's easy. They make friends by playing football...
...or discussing one of the things they like.
GLOOK

Football... films... video games...
...all their different wounds...
Yes. I've seen this. Watch, Mildred.

THBBB

Do you like ships with 400 guns coming out of them and shooting simultanously?

He's wandering off.
He seeks the company of his own kind.

Are you sure we shouldn't have spoken to him?
No! We'd have put the stink of girls on him.

The boys would have rejected him.
Pecked him to bits.

All right there mate, what's your name?

It's Lem. Would you like an onion?

Er no thanks, uh-

CRUNCH

...and if the ball hits the roof, 40 points to your opponent, Sonny.
Right... um... ok, Linton, ok...

Have you lads ever seen someone eat a raw onion like an apple?
Well, salads can have raw onion in them, Colm.

Yeah, but... I tried talkin' to that new kid.
Next thing you know...
ONION.

It might be for medical reasons!
Have you EVER heard of anyone having to eat onions as medicine?

I'll go and say hello.

Eh, now, you were bound to eventually meet someone who didn't like you, so.
I'M CRYING BECAUSE OF THE ONION!

TRICKS

Well look at that. He's made a couple of friends.
They look like they're having a great time, don't they.
Just staring straight forward.

Yeah what's with th-
LOTTHIE! LOTTHIE!

AAAH! A wasp!
That ithn't *funny*.

Sorry Little Claire.
Mrs Lord ith here. She'th in the clath room!

Arrived a week late! The *shame of it!*
She'th NOTHING like you imagined! NOTHING!
Come thee!

I'm so excited that I'm *vibrating!!!*
HMMM.

It's weird not being in the same class as Lottie any more.
We'd been in the same class since we were 4!!

Well you couldn't have gone all the way to the old folks home together.
And you've still got Mildred.

Mildred's Lot-tie's friend. We don't really have a lot to talk about.

You must do. Can't you both just fill in for half a Charlotte?
WOLF

Mildred I have... um... so much gossip for you that my... *feet feel hot?*
SWIP

Me too!

Jack, you've got the wisdom...
...of a much older woman.
LEAN

Class, I'm Mrs Lord. I want to apologise for not being here last week.
It was due to the unstable political situation in the Middle East.
MRS LORD

I took care of it.
LORD
HELLO 1971.

There's so much make up and hair and perfume, my eyes won't focus.
I like her! I *long* to be *lordly!*
C
G

Lotthie what do you think of the new boy?
He looks like a chicken that came out of the egg too soon.
CHEW
CHEW
RENEWABLE ENERGY
G

And he stinks of ONIONS.
Yeth! Thomeone should tell him.

Paper rock thissors to dethide who.
SNIP
Fetch the magnifying glass then, Little Claire.

I've well got no clue what those dainty little hands are up to.

Where's Lottie? Is she coming with us to try on tops?
She's meant to be. Maybe 2L got kept back.

No look, she's down there already.

Lottie where are you going? Aren't you coming to the shops?
I've got to go.

Did we say something to *offend* her?

I don't think you CAN offend her!
She's so cheerful that one time they sent her to the doctors for it.

THE ROBIN HOOD
GARY THE HORSE
Has Lottie got a hobby we don't know about?
There's not much we don't know concernin' Lottie.
On account of her MOUTH.
JOHN RHE

Why would she just go off like that? And with the new kid?
Do you think Lottie's gone BAD?
Mildred, you don't "go bad" after a week.
GALLERY YARD

My big brother went bad after a whole summer hanging out on the rec...
...with lads who smoked and had knives.

And he was only bad when he was out and about with them.
Yeah, I bet your mum would have given him a clout.

TING
Heh yes you don't mess with Mum.

open
Could she have... *become a woman?*

No, that already happened.
She made us a pamphlet to celebrate.
Tamsin you are a woman now
ALAS I CANNOT GO SWIMMING TODAY FRIENDS
WOW
SHES DIFFERENT

The Case of the Lonely One

Psst! Look! Out in the wild!
Helloooo

Are you two behaving yourselves?
Hihihi yes!
Always, Mr Beckwith!

Mrs Beck-with's got me doing the shop-ping.
MRS BECKWITH!

Dang, what is your fascination with her?

She rode her bike through the school once
She always calls the headmaster "Chuffy"
She has the best hair
AND TATTOOS

Er... yes. Those things are true. So how are you enjoying being in Mr Spink's class?
Permission to speak freely, sir?
TWEAK TWEAK

We suspect him of being mentile, sir.
We think- maybe he needs a nice quiet hobby, sir.

MISSING CAT
scratch
scratch

Heya Mildred!
Lottie! Me and Shauna wondered what was going on-

...with you... er, hello?
That's a nice blike.
SUPER MARKET
BLIKE?

Is he your boyfriend now?
No!
Because pet food isn't the only aisle in the supermarket

So why'd you bring the onion eater?
The whiff is stronger than ever!

He's a right good laugh once you get to know him! You'll see!
SQUEEZE
SUPER MARKET
Urrr... all right. Would you both like a drink and a biscuit?

No. We're fine.
CRUNCH
CRUNCH

CRUNCH
CRUNCH
GNAM

Dudes dudes dudes
GOSSIP BOMB INCOMING.

Apparently "onion Lem" lives on an onion farm...
...on Cobbler's ridge!

And right his mum and dad make him eat onions every meal and-
-and-

He's a right good laugh, Shauna.
You'll like him once you get to know him.

Onions are good for you.

CLIP CLOP CL
Good *morning* class!
GOOD MORNING MRS LORD.

TAP TAP
Thorry I'm late, thir.
Offithial buthineth!

Take the register for me, Steven.
I'm not in the mood.

There were two kindth of milk at the coffee shop Mrs Lord.
Tho I did a bit of each.
That's fine.

Barker?
Yes... *Steven*

I hate Mondays.

That Mrs Lord eh Ryan?
Oof if I were ten years younger...
If you were ten years younger WHAT? Go on.

I don't ruddy know. It's just one of those things that people say.

If I were ten years younger... I'd not make a funny noise every time I stand up.
SCRATCH SCRATCH
I love our little chats, Derek.

Mrs Lord, can I ENTREAT you to keep our pigeonhole tidy?
CRAM
Entreat all you like, Mr Knott.

WINK

GULP

Why aren't you playing with your fwends, Shauna?
Dollies and that.
Sigh.
I've got swimming tonight. I'm doing my *homework.*

I thought maybe you were trying to get closer to *role-playing club.*

UGH WHAT NO

Like you'll slowly edge down the table they won't notice you joined.
You're *amazing,* Linton.

R-really?
WHIP

You've actually managed to bore me MORE than my homework.

PLUS TEN charisma.
RATTLE

Just keep an eye on Mildred, she's been quiet the last couple of days.
They're growing up. Suddenly they have to keep EVERY-THING secret.

When they were noisy, at least you always knew what they were up to.

Tom, I'm really not sure about this new friend of hers.

He's a bit *wrong.*
So what do you want to play?

I don't know. I'm going to the toilet. You two decide.
You're the guest, you choose, Lem.

OW OW I've got something in my eye!!
Don't rub it, let me look!
SCUFF

You'll like me when you get to know me, Sonny...

I'm a right... good... laugh.

JACK!
ZEST

Corky.
Oh we get ONIONS? Great.

He could have silky football skills, Baxter. Give him a chance.

WOOF

MAN ON!

HA-CHA!
BOBBLE

Goal?
Well it's an own goal. That's... sort of a goal?

HANDBALL! PENALTY!
If you see the ball, pretend it's a bomb and RUN AWAY.
WHACK
PLUT

Sir, the score's 31-4, can you put Lem on their team please. *31-4.*
We're getting MURDERISED.
All right, swap sides with Corkindale.

Onions is so bad, he makes US look good, eh Corky.
Snuff, yeh.

How come you're doing games now?
I thought you had a "rolling sick note".
New family doctor.
JOG
JOG

First thing he does is ask me what football team I support.
You knew the good times were over, huh.

"Sport will do your weak chest good".
If exercise is so good for you, why do you never see DOLPHINS playing footer?
PUNT

Despite their superior intelligence, dolphins don't have the means to construct a leather sphere.
Ruddy dolphins. Got an answer for everything.

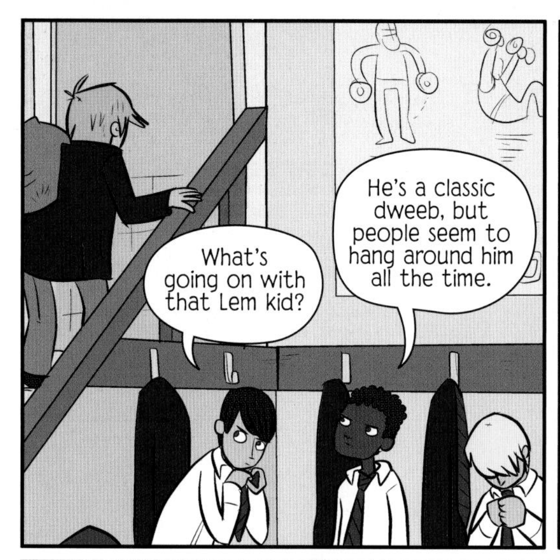
What's going on with that Lem kid?
He's a classic dweeb, but people seem to hang around him all the time.

Even Lottie and Mildred. It's *creepy*.
This feels like a MYSTERY!
Yes!

He's a right good laugh once you get to know him.

HA HA HA! That's exactly how they all say it!
Oh god, that's perfect.

Seriously though Sonny, something is going on.
Maybe his family is rich?

That doesn't explain why people have started eating raw onions like he does.
We'll get to the bottom of this boys.

Before his onion-crazy disciples fart the roof off the school.

NANG
MANG
GRANG

Message for you.
Jack, how many flipping love letters do you get a week?

JACK -
LET'S CLEAR THE AIR.
JUST YOU AND ME.
BACK LANE, 4PM.
LEM
It's not a "love letter" Linton.

Do you think he wants to fight me?
Human marshmallow vs the lollipop boy. I might try to sell the TV rights.

You're going home the wrong way, Jack.
I've got to meet Lem. To "clear the air".
I know, like, what?

That's no good! He's no good!
People don't seem RIGHT since he's been around.

What's he going to do, SCHLUB me to death?
Be *careful.*

Listen, if he's waiting with a cutlass or in full sumo gear, I promise to run away screaming.

GR

GRIT

GRIT

2

So did you fight? Did you punch the little freak in the guts?
NOT THAT I APPROVE OF THAT BEHAVIOUR.
No.

It turns out... he's a right good laugh.
Once you get to know him.

WHAT? HOW DID YOU "GET TO KNOW HIM"?
YOU WERE GONE FOR 3 MINUTES!
I'm going home now.

HEY! WAIT UP!

Why are people acting so weird?
What are you DOING to them?
SLAM

What if he's SICK, Shauna?
What if he tells people he's DYING, then they act weird?

I'm SO SORRY.
Here are your buttons.

All right lads, mystery meeting.
I've assembled the basic facts.

Since Lem Wake-field came to school, people are hanging around him like... Jack?

"Like flies around a dog tod", Jack, come on.
SCRIBBLE SCRIBBLE
This despite Lem having NO PERSONALITY.

"Lem-ites" (my own term) are dull and listless.
They begin to eat onions and claim-
LEM
LEMITES
WHY?
8

HE'S A RIGHT GOOD LAUGH ONCE YOU GET TO KNOW HIM.
Y-yes!

My plan is to follow him home and observe his ways in secret.
What do you think?
LEM
ITES
Behaviour
??
ONIONS

I think we should concentrate on our studies.
Yes, school is important.
Did you two get caught on the *naughty internet?*
MATHS
4
MATHS
4

Shauna, you have to help me.
It's Jack and Sonny, they're... *not right*...
I think LEM...

LINTON could you be any more *insensitive*?
He's, *you know!*
A BIZARRE FREAK?

Ugh, leave me alone!
AND GROW UP!
PUSH

Shauna!
SHOVE
Linton, we've discovered something!

Aw boys, phew! I knew I could rely on you.
It's in the back, here.

Onions is a secret were-wolf, right?
It'll blow your MIND.

Linton, there you are.
Sorry I was mean earlier, I-

Onions taste GOOD!
GRIND
ONIO

GLORF

CRUNCH
CRUNCH

NYAM
NYAM

GNAW
GNAW

Urr...
CRUNCH
GNAW
GRIND
GLORF
NYAM
NYAM

It's pretty unfair that it's ME who has to come up with an excuse here.

What the DICKENS is going on?
GLORF
GNAM
GNAW
GRIND

FWOOMP

We need to talk.
And not about how it is nice weather for DUCKTH.

The Case of the Lonely One

Rumour hath it that you put the beatth on Onion Lem.
Yeah but... I figured... maybe he's really ill? Dying? So...

He'th not dying! Hith cheekth are *ruddy with health.*

He doeth GAMETH and P.E! You can get off gameth with a COLD!

Also if he ith on the way out..
...it ith no excuse to turn everyone into a THOMBIE!
SLOT

A "thombie"?
Ohhhh...
Thombieth eat brainth, not onionth.

I reckon, you put the beatth on him again and-
-get expelled? Have a baby at 16?

You are a long term thinker, Thauna.
And that ith a *terrible* plan.

There he goes.
OK, so we need to work out how Lem maketh our friendth into THOMBIETH.

One of uth needth to obtherve how he doeth it.
Both of us, Claire.

No, if we both get caught it will be a DITH-ATHTER.
I am thmall-er, I can hide better.

If I get caught, you can tell the world. You're very THERIOUS.
No one believeth a word I thay.
IT'TH MY LITHP YOU THEE.

I don't want you to get caught!

BLUNT
I will defend myself with this dinner knife.
TWIP

Let's hope it doesn't come to that.
Sure, sure.
For their thake!

Can you help me find my thimble?
What?
I'll give you a quid.

His THIMBLE?
Good luck, Little Claire.

DEET
DEET
DEET
Is it valuable?
It's part of a set.
I dropped it through there.

Oh good graciouth
He'th a HYPNOTISER!

The thituation could not be any more dread!

TAP

Stop struggling, Claire. You're well too little and weak to resist.
COME TO YOUR THENTHES, LOTTIE!

Give me those.

Things are so much nicer when you're one of us.

GUTS

THTAY BACK!
BLUNT

Come on Little Claire. Don't be silly.
It's better this way.
SCRIT
SCRIT SCRIT
SCRIT
SCRIT

Oh
Claire.

What happened in here?

And what does this MEAN?

"Glasses"?

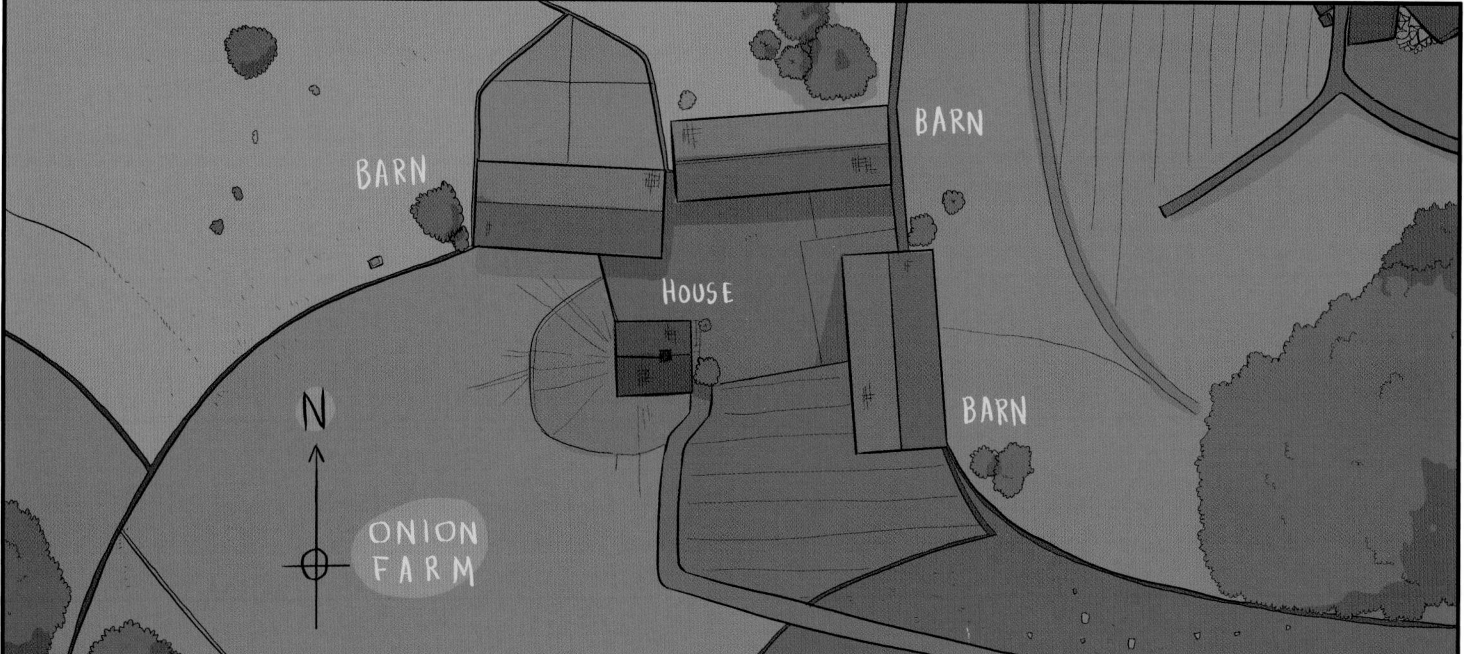
BARN
BARN
HOUSE
BARN
N
ONION
FARM

I want to stop, Mum. That last girl hurt me very much.
No more "making friends", Lem. We have enough of them.

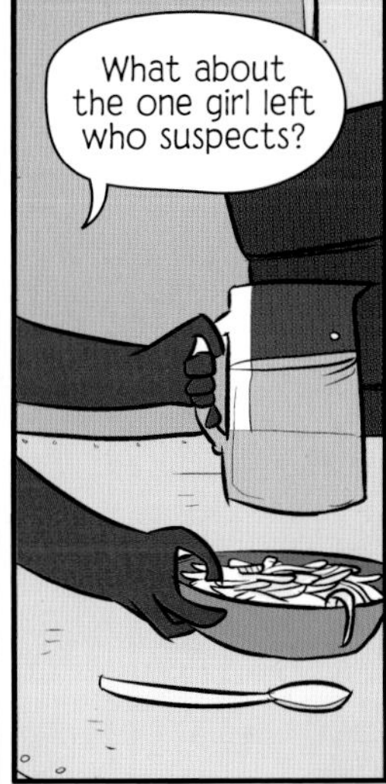
What about the one girl left who suspects?

She's got no one left to believe her. I took them all.
Adults will think she's just making it up.
FRESH ONIONS HONESTY BOX

A silly little girl.

Well done son. Eat up your onion bits and off to school.
I'M SICK OF ONIONS.

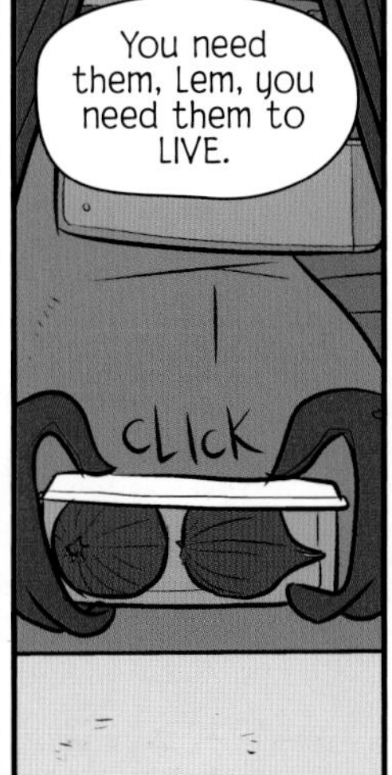
You need them, Lem, you need them to LIVE.
CLICK

I JUST WANT TO BE LIKE EVERY-ONE ELSE.

We know, son.
We know.

...I'll ask Ryan. Hey, Beckwith.
You can't have one of my Jaffa Cakes, man. You're a biscuit non-bringer-in.
BENSON'S
JAFFA CAKES
12

Are your class acting... *normally*?
Yeah, I think so.

There's a few criminals, but they're mostly law abiding.
Ours have gone mad, Mr Beckwith.

They don't CHAT. They don't SHOUT.
They all, always, do their home-work.

They eat a lot of fresh vegetables.

That sounds soothing, guys. Maybe they're all gettin' into yoga.
They never "get into" anything good for them.

I think the tuck shop might be contaminated with lead.
Hungry. Jaffa cake. A-a-a.
I'm takin' these home with me.

Where is he, that man of mine?

Take a picture, son. It'll last longer.
WINK!

Have you seen my wife? She's meant to be waiting for me.
I had my hair did! Do you like it?

Yeah! It's like I'm married to a new woman.
PRIMP

Fortunately she's the same height.
So I don't gots to adjust my "angle of affection".

I'm so impressed with the girls at your school.
Teasing-out hair like that takes time. It's an *art.*
That's Shauna Wickle. She's a good one.

But man, she don't look right of late.

There ain't much don't weigh heavy on slim shoulders, Ame.

Well thanks for that insight, *Cowboy Confucius.*
PWIP
CLICK

SAFË
BRIC A BRAC
108
BOUGHT + SOLD
108
OPEN
TUMBLE

Come in and *buy something.*
CAFE

COME IN. BUY SOMETHING.
SNAP

THEY CAN SMELL DESPERA-TION THROUGH THE WINDOW.
CAFE
CAFE

Customer customer customer customer
COME ON.

OMG OMG! SAD SCHOOLGIRL.

Do you need a hand, Mrs Beckwith?
TOTTER

CLOG

Thanks! I'd probably have been badly crushed.
Let me get you a cup of coffee as a reward...?

Shauna. Well Mrs Beckwith I don't really drink cof-
"Amy" please. "Mrs Beckwith" is my mother-in-law.

Coffee is rocket fuel for your mind, Shauna.
It's very good for you.
Don't most rockets *explode?*

zzt
zzt
lick
lick
zzt

TWINK

I can hear the clock ticking
I told you coffee was good stuff. Would you like some more?
JIG
JIG
JIG

I'm not sure.
They do a cup bigger than your head.
It feels like it lasts forever.

Hey, what's the matter?
You can tell me. It goes no further.
I'm not going to write it on the toilet wall.

Well, not one that anyone you know's going to see.

I've fallen out with all my friends.
No one talks to me any more.
Oh no, Shauna! What did you do?
WINE BARN

Did you steal some-one's boy-friend?

No!
Does some-one someone else likes like you?

What? No!
I'm not a bad person, Amy! I don't understand what's going on!

All you can do is be a good person.
If you feel hard done to...

...don't take it out on the people on the next rung down, you know?
THAT'S IT! THAT'S IT!

108
Well either she's off to punch a nerd in the 20-sided dice-
-or she realised how out of depth I was and cut her losses.

TIM TIM TIM TUM

Hey you dropped something.
Shurrup Tuan, Wickle's well up herself.

A space marine!

This is a sign! A *signal!*
Huh. No drybrushin' at all.
She in't even done any *high-lights.*

Go NORTH.
You enter a castle keep. There's a bearskin rug on the ground and-

-giant pink llamas come flyin' out of your bum singin' LA CUCARACHA
Lightning bolt

If he stares at Shauna Wickle any harder, she'll catch fire.
Break enchantment

WHAT'S THIS ABOUT?
CLUMP

I had to get your attention.
Everybody in our year's acting strange except you three.
I need your help to find out why.

Haven't noticed. No one's messed with us in weeks.
Isn't *that* strange too?

Why should we CARE?

Why would we want to put things back how they were?
PLEASE! There has to be some-thing I can do to convince you!
Anything!

Two dates, three distinct hand holding walks.
One kiss in front of the school.

DEAL

Well *that* took a lot of ruddy thinking about.

Come on Blossom, come back over.
Shauna's got a plan.
SCRIBBLE SCRIBBLE

She in't one of us, Tuan.
She's usin' us, but you lads want to be used.

Well if you want, we could test her.
Yeah a test! Show her up as ONE OF THEM.

Dwarf.

Elf.

Chaotic good Paladin

Spendthrift Mage-Duke.

Wow! She's good! One of us!
Shauna's a MEGA SWOT! She's REVISED this!

That's two orcs you glued together and made a new head for out of a thimble.
SO UNFAIR.

ONION FARM

Son, we got you some invites for your party.
Yussss

Auugh WHAT?
They've got TEDDY BEARS on, these are BABY INVITES!

Bears are among the planet's deadliest animals!
Yeah, whatever, *sigh.*

Come To My Party
Your going down
Death to non bearz
Date
Time
SO EMBARRASSING

Party at Lem's on Saturday!
Did you get the invite?
YEAH!

Party at Lem's!
Party at Lem's!
I can't wait!

OHHH there's a party at Lem's, it's gonna be a time

When Lem says party, it's on his dime!
DANCE

With party hats on and horns a HOOTIN'

A cake made of taters if you can't eat GLUTEN

He's a right good laugh, you can't DENYYYY-

HEY, I thought every-one was going to start singing!
I hate you all.

It's so weird watching every-one being friends without me.
They've got new jokes I don't get.

Flipping Norah that was *well the most embarrassing thing I've ever done*

Oh that's right, just walk past me, "best friend".
Just because I shamed myself in front of everyone.

DRRIINGGG
I'll give you a punch after school for your crimes against *friendship.*
Lottie?

Onion, Lottie?
Auugh what no Claire!
YEATS

OWWW my head hurts

I think... I WILL have that onion after all.

That's the third time I've lost her.
She's got the attention span of a moth in a light-bulb factory.

3

PARTY DAY
L E M

Wow, no wonder Lem is weird...

...look at his parents!

I'd feel sorry for him if he wasn't a mad bodysnatchin' freak.
RUFFLE
AIR PORT

God where *are* they?
Is that them?

What took you so long? The party started 15 minutes ago!
Tuan couldn't find his-

KEYSWORD!
Right.
click

The thing about an excuse is, it's a *reason* you were late.
It's not just your lips saying words that don't mean anything.

Well, you're here now.
So we're going to sneak down to the onion farm...
...and see what the heckins is going on.

Any questions?
OW! OW OW OW!

I stung myself on a nettle! IT REALLY HURTS!
Rub a dock leaf on it, Blossom.
Don't be so flipping soft.

Ur hur hur hur hur!
This is PATHETIC! Stop BLUBBERING!

You aren't talking to us like that. Come on Tuan, we're off.
Wait! WAIT! Please!
THWACK
THWACK
THWACK

Don't worry, Wickle.
I believe I've just successfully taught myself kendo.
CRACK
WHIP

Line of sight, Wickle, line of sight.
Are you in the army cadets, Corky?
Because you don't seem the type.

Games. I play a lot of games.
I'm basically 97% combat ready thanks to gaming.

I don't really play shooting video games, I suppose they're quite, er, realistic?

Games now are about as realistic as they can get, you reckon, right?
But the next generation will be so real that people will get *confused.*

Like maybe people will accidentally strangle the postman thinking he's a zombie.
Or-
Hmm, do you know what would be nice?
SIDLE

If you could write all this down so I can read it a few times.
What.
Because I am *that fascinated.*

Auugh! Your hair gets everywere!
Shh! What's going on in there? They're just drinking pop!

What's mama onion saying?
AIR PORT

Whatever it is, Lem doesn't like it!
CRUNCH
AIR PORT

Where's he leading them? Where are they going?
Looks like into the cellar.

THE CELLAR?
It's a house of evil!
That's the ROOM OF DOOM!

What's THAT?
WOMMMMMMM

What's going to happen down there?
More brain-washing? Being made into *pies*?
Birthday cake and sandwiches?
MMMMMMMM

We have to do something! We have to BREAK IN!
W-what? But I'm going to be a lawyer and-
WOMMM

Do you want your dates, your three hand holdings and your pash?
USE THIS BRICK!

BWONG

WHAT?
Try the front door!
I should have said that first.

The front door won't open! There's not even a KEYHOLE!
RATTLE

These walls look like brick but they don't feel like it!
What is this place?
What do we DO?

BE BRAVE
SAY THE RIGHT THING
BE A HERO

I can stay and help until 6 o'clock but then I have to go home for my tea.

The vibrating's stopped.

They seem fine. They seem like they had a good time.
No surgical scars.

Something's wrong.

Maybe we're too old for party bags now.
No party bags.

And not everyone can afford party bags, maybe.

A mini-bag of Haribos, two lollipops and something from Claire's Accessories?
Come on.

They can afford shatter-proof windows and lockless doors.
And a big thing that goes WOMMMM
You're going to be late for your TEA.

So did you enjoy the party?
What did you do?
NAUTICAL ALLIANCE

We played a game!
It took ages, but it was fun.

I don't know what it was called. It was...
...like a jigsaw puzzle?

There wasn't really a winner... you all had to work together.

Naturally I was the best at it.
PIP PIP PIP PIP
OVOID

I think it might have been... educational?
That would of been a mean trick.

PFF! It was very tiring, Daddy!

I think that..
...went VERY well.
PAT
PAT

What are those looks for? Am I in trouble?

Why didn't you tell us about Mosstyn?

MOSSTYN? Who's "Mosstyn"?

I told you not to embarrass the girl.
I don't KNOW anyone called Mosstyn!

Whoever he is, you're going round his house for dinner tomorrow night.

It's nice to hear you've got a new boyfriend.
Although I did like your Jack.

Dinner? What BOYFRIEND?
Apparently he thinks the world of you!

He was very polite on the phone. Sounded very HANDSOME!
Wait oh NO not CORKY!

Now since we've not met this lad, I wanted to have a word about-

Dan, if Corky lays one finger on me, he'll... he'll...
...be seeing through his nose and wearing his bum as a beard.
GRAM-MM

Wow Shauna, look at the size of this place!

Stop doing your power glower or you won't get invited back.
DING DING

How about this?
I s'pose they'll just have to work with "dangerously feral".

Hello
Hello Shauna, Mosstyn's told us all about you.
Mossy, your guest is here!

She's delight-fully ghastly, like a little mongrel dog!
You know, sweet, but completely flea-ridden.

God these people are appallin'.
I'm gonna be as bad as possible.

Put my feet on the table.
Fart under his mum's toffee nose.

You like Daniel Libeskind's work, do you dear?
Oh!

Um he's all right

He's not doin' anything Frank Gehry can't do 100 times *better.*
But that's just my OPINION.

BALLS
BALLS
BALLS
BALLS

I may have judged her too quickly. She's rough around the edges but-

Elise, won't you be joining us for dinner?
I TOLD you, I'm going out with Cassandra and Fleur.

You NEVER LISTEN.

STOMP
STOMP
STOMP
STOMP
STOMP

SLAM

She's under a lot of pressure... with exams and all.
If I talked to my mum like that...
...she'd use me instead of the mop on the kitchen floor for a WEEK.

SUPER BALLS.

Oh my god, nuff cutlery.
Do I just use the ones I like the look of best?
Oh just use the ones you like the look of best, Shauna.
So Mosstyn tells us that you're top of the year academically.
Um well yes sometimes it's me and sometimes it's my... friend Mildred.
Mildred's better at sciences.
And you're part of the swimming team?
Well I'm just fast so I'm in the team.
Mossy, well, he struggles, don't you?
So how did you two become friendly?
NAM
NAM
We...we..
We helped an injured bird together.
It died though.

PERFECT
ON YOUR FEET CORKY! I haven't finished with you.
Wheeze
STEP
HOP
STEP

No he can't come to the phone right now.
He's dancing with his girlfriend.
BIP
BEEP
YEAH

Okay.

Shauna, now that we're going out-
Corky we are NOT GOING OUT.
STEP
STEP
STEP
HOP
HOP
STEP

This is one date off your deal.
Three hand holds, one date, one pash left.
I don't *fancy* you.

Are we... friends?
Associates.
Play your cards right, you might make it to *colleague*.

She's a credit to you. You're welcome back any time, Shauna.
Thank you for having me.

If you can make an impression on people like that, you'll go a long way.
I did my BEST not to.
I couldn't HELP it.

Your mum and I are very proud of you.
They had a special toilet just for washin' your bits.
It was EXHAUSTIN'.

Chris I wish I could ADOPT HER right now.
How did our Mossy attract a girl like that?

He spends most of his time in his room drawing dragons.
Miracles *do* happen.
I did think he'd end up with Blossom though.

I never really thought of Blossom as a *girl*.
More a very unhap-py cloud.

Bad Machinery, Volume Four

What are you doing here? Go away!
We just want to talk.

Don't try your hypno-trick, we worked out that it don't work through glasses.
BOK

Please don't hit me, please don't hurt me

This is like an out of body experience.
tremble

We're not going to hit you. Pull your-self together.

Geeze Blossom, he makes US look tough.

I mean, he makes *me* look tough.
SHAKE
SHAKE

It took some time, girls, but that was good swimming today.
Mrs Lord is it okay if I go back into the school to get my blazer?

The caretaker locks up in ten minutes, so be quick, Wickle.

TROT
TROT
TROT

Either move faster or be less FRAIDY, Shauna.
STOP
TROT
TROT
TROT

4 MON
OCTOBER
TROT
TROT
TROT
TROT
TROT
TROT
TROT

4 MON
OCTOBER
Shhhh

Someone's behind me!

Please! *Come on!*

You wouldn't do this to me!
Of every-one it could be, not you!

You thought you could use us, Shauna.
But things are better since Lem got here.

Now you're going to say "he's a right good laugh once you get to know him", right?
SQUIRM

Actually he's really, really boring.

If he's not hypno-tized you, then I don't understand why you're doing this.
We have to STOP him!

We're not all like you, Shauna. Thin and pretty and in the swimming team.
AND YOU DON'T LISTEN.

I told you, since Lem started changing people, no-one messes with us any more.
In't that right, TUAN?

You sold me out!

You maybe sold out the WHOLE PLANET...
...because you wouldn't stand up to people who teased you.
TUG
The whole p-planet?

HOLD ONTO HER!

Come on, do your thing Lem.
She's too kicky!
She'll hurt me!

I'm sure the whole planet's quaking in its boots.

This is WRONG, Blossom!
Tuan!

Get off me, you stupid-
SCUFFLE

-COW
BARGE
SHOVE

CRACK

FLOP

He's not breathing! He's dead!
This is your FAULT! Your fault, Blossom!

CHIK CHIK
Does that really matter?
Everyone knew you hated him.

CHIK
That's why no one talks to you any more.
You pushed him, he fell.

We saw her go for him, didn't we Tuan?
Or were you... IN ON IT?

BLAM

Good-night Wickle!

That girl's dedication to fitness is *inspiring*.

We're locked in, Tuan.
My mum and dad'll go mad.
I wish we could put the lights on.
RATTLE
RATTLE

He's coming to bits. Is that normal when somebody dies?
How would I know?
ROLL

AHURRRRRK

He's making noises. Is that normal when somebody dies?
I think we should sit somewhere else.
TAP TAP TAP TAP

God I promise I will be a good person if I don't have to go to jail for Lem dying.
I promise I will spend my life helping people.
And if Lem could still be alive-

OOO EEEEOOO

GOD PLEASE DON'T LET MUM AND DAN FIND OUT IT WAS ME.
Amen.

Shauna love you look terrible.
I didn't get much sleep.

Well have some breakfast.
I can't. I've got to get into school early.
Project.

I love you, Mum.
HUG

Shauna! Shauna!
I had some ideas about Lem and-

Just hold my hand
And shut the flip up until we get to school.

Well Mr Bough I never seen anything like it in thirty years.
The two of them in there all night, and the MESS!
S

Bits of onion everywhere, there was.
Move along, sticky beak!
Sorry Mr Bough!

SIDDOWN CLASS.
I have a note here from the deputy head.

Onions are now forbidden on school premises.
AWWWW
HERBIE

Are we allowed onion bhajis, sir?
What about shallots?
ECCE ROMANI 2

Pipe *down*, Haversham.

Sir?
What about *chives?*

Haversham, what's the nominative plural present participle of 'currere'?
HAVERSHAM?

Mildred

Haversham, are you making it your mission to aggravate my stomach ulcer?

What's that you're writing?
SNATCH

What is this? Experimental poetry in the style of ee cummings?
On your feet! EXPLAIN YOURSELF!

Sir I don't know sir
PETRONIUS
THRUST
I don't know what this is!

LIAR! SATURDAY DETENTION!

Currentes, currentia, sir.
Wickle, you've restored my faith in womankind.
PETRON
CRUNCH

He's had a dificult time but he's through the worst of it.
Oh my poor baby boy.

Our window is closing! We can't afford to coddle him.
He needs to be AT SCHOOL.

Yes but-
This is VITAL
Can we get a cat?

I don't feel good! *I don't wanna go to school!*

Lem we need you to bring your friends to another party. Just one more.
Then we can go home.

LEM come out of your cranny IMMEDIATELY.
NO.

Why has no one come for me yet?
Where are the police?
But at that point Kira relinquishes the death note and-
I HAVE TO CONFESS

Corky last night I-

HE'S ALIVE? AM I GOING MAD?

HOIST
Is this my pash?
Be gentle with me, Shauna.

Detention? I've NEVER had detention.

What did I write on that paper?
FISH
FISH
FISH

I must have developed a split personality.

AND SHE'S COMPLETELY MENTILE
Exclude non onion eaters
Never reveal the secrets of
the onion farm
Lem is a right good laugh
once you get to
Onions are delicious
Exclude non onion
Never reveal the
the onion

Saturday detention, can you flipping believe it?
Is this another trick to trap me? I'm sick of it! Sick of you all!

Oh give it a rest Shauna, I've got a banging headache.

Prove you're not one of Lem's onion zombies NOW.

Or I am going to sit and be sad somewhere else.

FURTIVE MOVEMENT

I've drawn on a second set of eye-brows in permanent marker.

I AM SO 4 REALS, SHAUNA!

I don't know what to say.
I AM TWICE AS SERIOUS AS ANY HUMAN HAS EVER BEEN.

I'm going to have to get these off with *turpentine*.
That's what the Victorians used to wipe the *face* off the *moon*.
SCRUB SCRUB SCRUB
How did you break free?

I don't know! Beaky gave me that big telling off in Latin.
THE SHAME OF IT
And suddenly you were the old you again?

I saw Lottie in the corridor one day... NORMAL.
Next time I saw her, zombie again,
OUI
NON

Wait, was it the day Lem gave out his party invitations?
She stood on a table and sang a mad song that day with music only she could hear.
scrape

Everyone just stared. She was WELL embarrassed. *Mortified*!

EMBARRASSMENT BREAKS LEM'S SPELL!

Go over them with concealer, but make it look natural.
I'm aimin' for *natural-ish*.

Right, so how are we going to embarrass everyone to freedom?
I thought steal all their clothes while they're in the showers after games.
PAT PAT
PLAN

Shauna you are thinking *small.*
We have to go BIG, stop whatever madness is going on at Lem's farm.

You were there, Mildred, what did you all do in the cellar?
It wasn't a cellar! It was HUGE!

Lem's mad old mum and dad had us crawling inside some machine and fixing it.
TAP TAP
It was hard, I got so many scratches, but Lem kept telling us it was... fun?

What sort of machine? A washing machine?
No, bigger, Shauna.
A washer-dryer?

Party at mine on Saturday, we've just got a trampoline.

Party at mine. Trampoline.

Trampoline.
Trampoline!
TUCK
GNAM

Mildred this isn't going to work.
Listen to me, go up to Lem and say sorry.
Say it like you *mean* it.

All he wants is to fit in. He wants REAL friends.
But he's SCARED of me!
PARTY

He wants your approval more than anything.

Look, I've got detention so I can't go to his trampoline party. You have to...
...eat CROW, Shauna.
FLAP
FLAP

Eat the whole crow if you have to.
BONES, BEAK and ALL.
SHOVE

Lem, I just wanted to say sorry for everything.
I hope we can be friends. No more stupid fighting.

Now I've got to know you...
TR . . . UCE?
I think you're a right good laugh.

Make her eat a raw onion.
Including the skin.

Bones, beak and all, Shauna.
Bones, beak and all.

Pretend it's an apple, *pretend it's an apple.*
GNAM

BLAH
BLEH
BLEH
BLEH
BORG
BLOGH
BLAH
BLEH

Ha ha hahahah
HA HA HA!!
SPIT
PTUI
PTUI
PTUI

Party at mine on Saturday.
THRUST
We've just got a trampoline.

PLACE
Is your coffee working?
I'm feeling quite jangly.
8.50! I have to get a move on!

A-PPARENTLY they kick you out of Saturday detention at 12.
So I'll be at Lem's by *one*.
WHOK
Write down your observa-tions until then.

I'm scared Mildred!
Me too! Satto detto is full of school's most hardened criminals.
I've got to live through that to get down to how scared *you* are.

Flipping Norah. Worst of the worst.

Filled some-one's bag with lab gas.

Sold her mum's ciggies in the loos at break.
POLDERS

Drew a willy on the bonnet of Mr Peebles' new car.

Hid in an organ pipe, no one knows why.

I think your work is really groundbreaking!

This is it, the last day we have to look out at... all of this.
The children will be here soon, put on your disguise.

I never thought this day would come.
It's been... so LONG.
No more grubby little humans on their grubby little world.

Lem! Get dressed for your guests!
SCOOT

FIRE MOVIE
PWOING

You know, 90% of childhood injuries are caused by trampolines.
PWOING

Do you want a go?
FIRE MOVIE

YES.

Come on in, Shauna.
FIRE MOVIE
PANDA POP

You look... terrible, Lottie.
HEY WHAT my sister got me this tshirt in BROOKLYN.

She says Brooklyn is well good, it's the home of fashion and COOT-YORE ideas.
People will just rock up in a suit of armour and a tutu and-
IMPRACTICAL GOODS SINCE 1999
WORLD OF NEW BANDS
BOOM BOXES INC
ONE WAY

I mean you're almost *grey*. You *all* look *ill*.

How many onions have you been eating a day?
ONIONS ARE DELICIOUS

Yeah right, very more-ish. How many?
I donno, twenty? They're well cheap.

You've been living on onions?
YOU'VE BEEN LIVING ON ONIONS?
COUNT

Lem, what have you done to these children?
MUSIC IS AMAZING, JACK.
FIRE MOVIE

What's going on?
Lem's getting a right doing.

Human children can't live on onions!
I DON'T SEE WHY I should be the only one who has to

Everyone called me a FREAK
But now onions are COOL

CREEEAK

I HATE YOU BOTH! I HATE YOU!

There are only a few hours left..!
I'll go after him, you have the children move the engine.

Who wants lemonade? This way!
Yeah.
I don't feel well.
Have an onion.
GORK

These people are like a jigsaw with bits missing.
BOOKS NOT BOYS

If they've got a masterplan, I've got a monkey for a butler.

AAH!

Halloween costumes! Weird.

This place goes on forever! But it's a WRECK!
Everything looks like it came off a scrap heap.
Maybe these people are just eccentric.

But what about Lem's hypnotising?
Is he doing it all on his own?

And if he is, we've worked out how to beat him! *Embarrassment!*
We've foiled his schlubby plan and-
BRUSH

AAAAAAAAAAAAAAAAAAAAA

BREATH

AAAAAAAA

Pris... pris...
Habba habba
scroff
Koko
shuff
GORK
totter

Move, Shauna
MOVE

HAVE TO STOP SCREAMING
GOING TO BLOW A GASKET

Only one option...
BAAHWWW
LET IT ALL OUT IN ONE MEGA SCREAM!

Get away from me! Get away!
PUSH

Please don't hurt them! Please!

It's just a can of hairspray!
BOOKS NOT BOYS

It's only hand-bag size!

You were meant to think...
...it was pepper spray
OH GOD

ONION BABIES

SO CUTE

WANNA KISS THEM ALL

Bok gokkko aaugh
No listen it's just a can of hairspray, it's-
BOOKS NOT BOYS

SHAUNA STOP TRYING TO BE GOOD FOR ONCE IN YOUR LIFE
YOU'RE WINNING

Tell me what's going on in this house, all right?
NOW!

Urrrgh! Auugh!

Or I'll spray up your babies...
STIFF AS BOARDS!

Oh no no no please don't CRY!
Oh no shhh shhh shh

It's empty, I ran out see?
Stop SCUTTLING!
SCUTTLE
FUT

My wife and I are from the planet Korfus.
It is more distant than you could possibly imagine.
I AM WELL INTO THIS.

Having detected intelligent life on your planet, we were part of a diplomatic mission.

We set off hundreds of years before our intended arrival, and traveled in suspended animation.

Based on Veffus' Law, we calculated that by 1955, your race would have evolved to reach a peaceful utopia...
...as Korfus had existed for millennia.
As we awoke from our long sleep, we discovered that Veffus' Law was *faulty*.

Yeah because humans still LOVED fightin'?

No. We discovered that our own planet had been destroyed...
...in "The Battle Of Whose Turn Is It".

You'd better not be joking me. *I'm 13.*
I'm not *stupid*. I wrecked these eyes *READIN'*.

On entry to earth's orbit, our pilot lost control of the vessel...

And we crashed here on the onion farm.

But Earth's strong gravity and the after-effects of suspended animation left us feeble....

...and most of the crew were slain by the farmer's wife with a shovel.

HUMANS ARE BARBARIC OH GOD!

Wait did you crash the space ship on the FARMER

I... don't remember...
SHAME ON YOU
VORT

I thought this was a party, Sonny.
Instead, Lem's mad ole mammy has us draggin' god knows what god knows where.
DRAG

I think she's going through the MEN-TAL-PAUSE.
My gran's always going on about it.

It's where an old bird's brain overheats and she starts collectin' royal family plates.
Stickin' them on the wall.
USHER
USHER

Thank flip being an old man just means bein' addicted to toffee.
GRRRK
WHOMP

AAUGH MY TUMMY AWWWW
Get up! Get up! We're almost there.
Sorry Lem's mum, I'm just going to have a lie down too.
FARRRRT
FART FART
GRRRRRK
PARP

My guts are at WAR.
I'm on Google...
...lemonade and onions cause...
GRRRORK
BLORP
BLORP
BLORP
LIFE THREATENING TRAPPED WIND!

Let's play a STANDING UP GAME!

The farmer's wife... ran away...
YEAH RIGHT OKAY

...and ever since we've been building an escape vehicle.

But we were weak. Progress was so slow.
We needed human help, but we couldn't reveal ourselves and our technology.

So you sent your son to get children to help?
But he's not... like you...

The farm was abundant with life! Onion life!
My wife and I were scientists, we used what we had!

You GREW a son?
He had to look human. He was not our first attempt.
GOGGO

Exceptional solar activity this afternoon will power our ship launch and-

UM is Lem meant to be pulling all those wires out?

WANG
WANG
WANG
WANG
WANG
WANG
What are you doing?

I'm gonna smash it it! Gonna smash it so we don't have to leave!

Lem! No son! We're going home!
This is my home
PULL
FIRE MOVIE

He's pretty weak. He's just scratched this panel a bit.

But why do you want to go home, isn't it partially destroyed?

We just want to feel light again before we... we...
To feel light again.

Are you... are you... um, pretty old?
LEM WILL YOU KNOCK IT OFF!?
WANG
FIRE MOVIE

Why have you stopped moving the engine?
The children! The children! *They're broken.*
BARP
BAR
BROKEN!?!
BOOKS NOT BOY

I've blown up like a dead sheep in a river, Shauna!
I *told* you! Onions are a *sometimes food*!
GORK
BOOKS NOT BOYS

We've not long until take-off.
I tried to move it. It's too HEAVY for just us.
01001

This is just a physics problem! *Basic physics!*
I thought you were scientists!
FIRE MOVIE

You managed to fly through space and grow onion babies!

Our minds... we're... NOT YOUNG.
Well I don't know... I...
SLUMP

Ngh! I don't GET IT.
Shauna I thought you wanted to be an architect! Come on!
Basic physics!

MILDRED! We need MILDRED!

Come on bus, *come on.*
TAP
TAP
TAP
TAP

BRAMMMM

SPRINT

Where is that blonde phantom?

Where is she?

Where are those Saturday felons at?

A light on! Must be the detention room!
SPRINT

Mildred, you're different from the other 2nd year girls.
Taller? I'm tall for my age.

Mildred laaaa!

Anytime you're ready.
Anytime.

So that's Satur-day detention eh? PASHING ON 4th year boys!
Mr Carter nicked off for an emergency after 20 minutes.
DRAG
BOOKS NOT BOYS

I'll probably never get to kiss anyone EVER AGAIN Shauna.

I'll be known as Mildred Haversham, KISS-LEAVER.
Those bad kids would've led you into a life of crime.

They lived life fast. They stayed up late.
They'd made moody faces into an art form.
WEEK

Okay so this is what you want?
C. Huzzah
ROCKET
B. Rocket takes off
A. Engine pushed into hole in rocket
engine

We will achieve this using BASIC PHYSICS.

My friends are bravely stomping hundreds of onions into a thin, watery paste.
SQUIT
SQUIT
SQUIT
HATE ONIONS NOW!
MY GUTS, MAN!

Like a train compressing autumn leaves on rails, this will create...
...a TEFLON-LIKE NON-STICK COATING ON THE GROUND.

Using the last of their strength, they will push the engine into the "skid zone"
It will GLIDE into position.

Do you think this will work?
Well, Mildred seems very sure of herself.
But she was very sure that *"the queen can just shoot anyone she likes"* too.
STOMP
STOMP
STOMP
STOMP
STOMP
STOMP
STOMP

1-2-3
CHARGE!

SLAM

GLIDE

It worked! It's sliding into place! Like a...RACING SLUG!

Come on, you've got to go!
Thanks Shauna, thanks for everything!
MOVIE

Initiating launch sequence! Is everyone ready to go?

I'm not going back to their stupid planet.
This is my home. With my friends.

SCOOCH
I don't need them. They just USED me.

LIFT OFF!
CLICK
Hurray!
Gok gok!

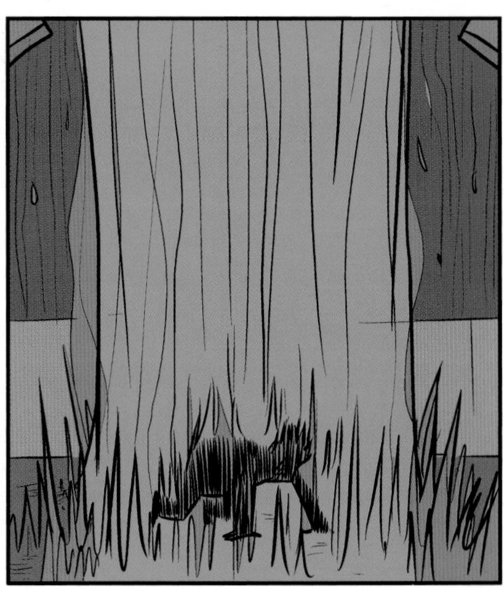

Where's... *Lem?*
FLIP
FLIP

Bad Machinery, Volume Four

What he's saying... that he grows back? Makes sense.
Little Claire kicked him right in the middle fighting him off.

HURK
HUKK
HUKK
First he couldn't breathe, then he flaked off a layer and he was fine.

Or, you know, fine for *Lem.*
I think he's hurt worse than he can flake off this time.

Are you still there? I'm cold.

Yes! I just wanted to say, um...
...you were a right good laugh... *once I got to know you.*

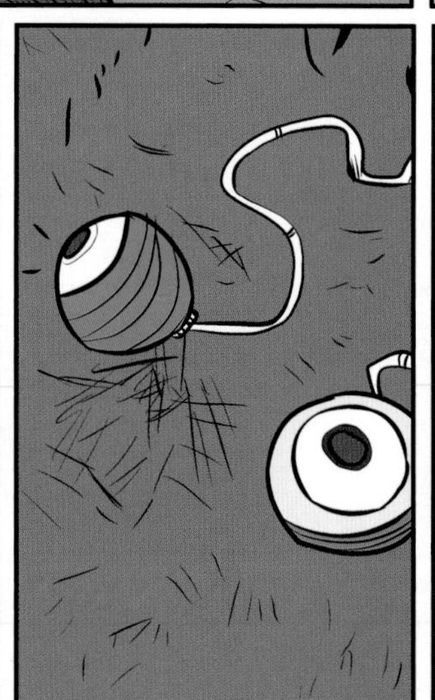

I'm sick of this stupid place.
Let's go home.

Don't get hypnotised, Mildred!
Don't worry.
I don't think they've got a lot of go left in 'em.

What I want to know is why Lem's mum and dad didn't just use them to hypnotise NASA...
... to build them a rocket.
Wow man. The hyp-no-eyes.

The dad said that adults notice when other adults are actin' mad.
But kids do nutty things all the time.

Not us. We're well sane.
Here's fine. Let's bury them.
RIP

Shauna, we're sorry we were bad to you when we were hypnotised.
It was horrible. But I forgive you.

Don't ever do it again.

We have to *double* say sorry to Little Claire.
She fought us like a mad beetle to help you.

Oh it'th fine.
I'm thure it wath character forming.

So she fixed every-thing without me. The whole Lem business.
HUH.

Come sit with us for lunch, yeah Corky?

Just let me get my sandwiches

Blossom!
Where do you think you're going?

Shauna told me what you did, tried to trap her in the school with Onion Lem.

Shauna Wickle is a pram-face council estate SKIPPER.
She *lies*. She lied to you Corky, lied about every-thing.

Where's Tuan? What's a "skipper"?
His mum took him out of school.
And I don't know but it *sounds right.*

Shauna locked me and Tuan in the school to get us in trouble, then told us to keep away from you.
LEM WASN'T THERE.

Now everyone's looking at me and whispering.
It's not FAIR.

We've been friends a long time.
You've known her 5 minutes.
But-

She said she could "have anyone she wanted".
Who do you believe?

What would a girl like that want with you?

She and her mates just want to laugh at you behind your back.
PRIMP

I'm your *real friend.*
I know.
I've got my tuba lesson. See you in History.

CHEW
CHEW
CHEW
CHEW
CHEW
CHEW
CHEW
There he is!

Where were you at lunch? We waited!
I don't want any-thing to do with you.

What? Why?
SPELLCASTING: REPEL VERMIN

OH MY *LORE!*
HAHA HAHAH!

PORKs
So you think Lem just onioned himself back to life after he fell down the stairs?
I reckon. And legged it away home. You can't even lock school doors from the inside.

I did not know that Shauna.
That is a good fact worth writin' down.

There's something wrong with that Blossom.
We will watch out for her. Good and close.
And for Mildred, who is noticing boys and getting NOTICED.

She's not little and loud now. She's sort of... *willowy?* Willowy.

She snuck into teens without tellin'. September 1st. Under the RADAR.
And you go teen tomorrow!
I'm a poor July baby.

Still a wiggler and an egg when you popped out.
I miss being little and loud, Lottie.
PLONK

If we can't be little any more...
...we'll make up for it by being LOUDER.
HUG

THE MOSSY TRAVELLER
Corky turned down the big hair queen of the second year?
I'm tellin' you Spinky, it happened just like that.
Cussed Shauna Wickle with a D&D spell.
He'll regret that for the rest of his life.

I think you need a brain to regret some-thing, Abi.

Cussed with a spell.
Like putting all your savings in the Bank Of Future Embarrassment.

BORT

It's YOU! Where have you been?

EVERYWHERE.

THE END

SKETCHBOOK

The way I write my stories is always changing, but I prefer to do most of the work with pencil and paper if I can. Writing things out longhand means I can draw alongside my notes, try out visual jokes, rough out characters, and work anywhere without needing my computer or a power outlet, away from distractions. I wrote most of this story on trains in cheap square sketchbooks. Here are some of my favourite rough drawings and what I remember about writing *The Case Of The Lonely One*.

LITTLE CLAIRE

I introduced Little Claire in the last case as a fun character (admittedly, a fun character who has a slight problem with pyromania). I still thought of her that way until she started helping Shauna. Although she's little, she's not fragile. People underestimate her in almost every *Bad Machinery* case.

SHAUNA

This is the first *Bad Machinery* story where one mystery solver has to do it (almost) all on her own. Shauna is one of the quieter characters, but I think that made this case more interesting. Juggling six characters often means that the sensible ones keep the plot moving while the nutty ones deliver some hot jokes. Leaning on someone who couldn't just fool around while being abandoned by all her friends meant that I had to change how I told a story. Anything that forces me to not to be lazy is good.

CORKY'S HOUSE

Drawing fancy houses is a treat. I go on real estate websites, type in a price that I could never afford, and have a snoop around all the photos. It's free fun! Don't judge me!

BLOSSOM, CORKY & TUAN

When I start drawing a story, the details for the later parts are very loose, so that anything that occurs to me as I'm working can be slotted in. This often means that characters who start with small parts get built up if they work well.

Tuan, Corky and Blossom didn't even have names when I started, but they all got their own little backstories. Cork and Tuan play as standard nerds, but Blossom is my favourite of the three. Nobody is going to mess with her and get away with it. She's a much more formidable enemy for Shauna than poor pitiful Lem the onion boy.

THE ONION FARM

I grew up next to a farm. On the plus side, the neighbouring field often contained the same animal you were eating for your dinner, which bred a healthy respect for "livestock". On the downside, one was regaled by some of the most ferocious biological odours imaginable if the wind was blowing in the right (wrong) direction.

MRS LORD

Mrs Lord was just a name in my notes for this story until the day before I had to write her first scene. I think she's the sort of person who no one has ever said "no" to. I had a little drawing of a French actress in my sketchbook. "That'll do", I thought.

THE MYSTERY KIDS

The mystery kids change a little bit in every story, but this is the story where the girls start to become little women. They're trying on slightly more sophisticated ideas for size, while the boys are probably still swapping stickers and throwing loose debris at each other.

On the first day of the second year of grammar school, I remember seeing the new intake, and they looked almost impossibly little. A year ago, that had been us. Social norms and rules and expectations seemed to change so fast during that time that you were never sure what was right and wrong. I think I spent about 50% of the second year of big school absolutely livid, burning furiously with embarrassment.

LEM: EVOLUTION OF ONION BOY

Lem's design came quite easily. Initially, he was meant to be very bland and forgettable, but then I remembered a boy at school who got home haircuts for a bit longer than was probably appropriate. His mother would neatly cut it into a pudding bowl shape, but the natural directions of his hair would turn it into what looked like three haircuts fighting on top of his head. Lem's rounded gait was inspired by the classic shape of a shallot.

HYPNO EYES

Is there a more magical mesmeric trope than the time-honoured hypno-eyes? From Kaa the snake onwards, nothing says "you are under my power" like a spiral. In fact, it's possible to be hypnotised by almost anything spiral shaped. Queen Victoria was famously put into a three-week hypnotic trance just by riding a helter-skelter at a funfair.

MEET THE PARENTS

I'm particularly fond of Lem's parents, Vizier and Empyrean. I don't think I ever used their names in the comic, so there they are. They're pretty old to be parents, and constantly exhausted by their teenage son. When you want to fit in, as Lem does, no one seems more out of touch with how you feel than your poor parents. When a child becomes a teenager, a parent goes from steering the ship to gripping onto the wheel for dear life and trying to stop the vessel from crashing into a series of ever more dangerous obstacles. And that's when the parent isn't an ancient alien hiding in a wrecked spaceship under a decrepit onion farm.

AMY

In the other *Bad Machinery* books, Amy Beckwith-Chilton doesn't really interact with the mystery kids. She only sees them from a distance, the way you or I might safely view a wasp's nest. Like a lot of adults, she's gone from being a child, to not being a child, to forgetting how to talk to children, to being actively afraid of children. It's a very normal, natural process—like puberty. Children are our future, they will replace us one day, turning our bones into gasoline for their futuristic cars. The fear is entirely justified.

But Amy sets aside the terror of being used to power a flying car by Shauna and takes her under her wing. It's an important day for both of them: the first day that Shauna enters the world of adults on equal terms, and the first time in years that Amy meets a teenager without crossing the street (or crossing herself).

Amy's look in this book is out-there and all over the place. I saw her kicked-out hair, her crazy jacket and her fluffy skirt walking down the street one day and scrawled them down as fast as I could. It was a look that said "confidence", but confidence is just armour for a fragile soul. It's hard to make new friends as an adult, you have to seize the chances when you can. I like Amy and Shauna as friends.

MR SPINK

My Latin teacher was a lot like Mr Spink. He was a short man, but every cell of his body was packed with a raw fury that he would unleash upon anyone who got anything wrong in class. He got results: you felt almost religiously compelled to cram the most obscure details of classical grammar and vocabularly into your unreceptive mind. So long as you never got anything wrong, he was quite pleasant. But there was no margin for error, he was wound tighter than a clock spring. He also worked as a barman in a local pub. A pub where, I assume, no one spoke without raising their hand.

ONION BABIES

I'm not a geneticist, but I'm ABSOLUTELY CERTAIN that if you tried to create an onion that could walk, talk and gibber, your early efforts would look like the onion babies. They're probably not even babies, are they? They're just small. The same size as an onion. "John, why onions?" you may ask, and the answer is simple. Setting it at a horse farm would have made the story much harder to draw.

JOHN ALLISON

Born in a hidden village deep within the British Alps, John Allison came into this world a respectable baby with style and taste. Having been exposed to American comics at an early age, he spent decades honing his keen mind and his massive body in order to burn out this colonial cultural infection.

One of the longest continuously publishing independent web-based cartoonists, John has plied his trade since the late nineties moving from *Bobbins* to *Scary Go Round* to *Bad Machinery*, developing the deeply weird world of Tackleford long after many of his fellow artists were ground into dust and bones by Time Itself.

He has only once shed a single tear, but you only meet Sergio Aragonés for the first time once.

John resides in Letchworth Garden City, England and is known to his fellow villagers only as He Who Has Conquered.

—Contributed by Richard Stevens III

"THE TREASURE OF BRITANNIA"